**BOOK REVIEW**

*Many economical words are briskly
exchanged before the happy ending.*
from SATURDAY REVIEW

Weekly Reader Books presents

An EARLY I CAN READ Book

ALBERT
THE ALBATROSS

Story and pictures by SYD HOFF

HARPER & ROW, PUBLISHERS

NEW YORK AND EVANSTON

ALBERT

THE ALBATROSS

Albert was a bird.

He lived on the ocean.

He was an albatross.

5

Sailors liked to see him.

An albatross is good luck.

They were happy

when Albert followed their ship.

One day there was a storm.

The wind blew and blew and blew.

The sailors could not see Albert.

Albert could not see the sailors.

All he could see was the land.

"Have you seen the ocean?"

Albert asked a bird in a cage.

The bird was a parrot.

"Polly wants a cracker," said the bird.

"Have you seen the ocean?"

Albert asked a bird in a clock.

The bird was a cuckoo.

"Cuckoo-cuckoo," said the bird.

"Have you seen the ocean?"

Albert asked a bird in a tree.

16

The bird was a woodpecker.

"Tap-tap-tap," said the bird.

"Have you seen the ocean?"

Albert asked a bird on a church.

The bird was made of tin.

It could not say anything.

19

Albert flew into a store.

"I want this one for my trip,"

said a lady.

"What a pretty hat," said her friends.

"That bird looks real."

22

"Thank you," said the lady.

"I will wear it on the ship."

The people got on the ship.

Everyone waved good-by.

"Good-by," said the lady.

It was time for dinner.

"I know you!" said the captain.

"No, you don't," said the lady.

"Not you," said the captain.

"I know the bird on your hat."

27

"Oh!" said the lady.

"I don't want a real bird on my hat."

"We want a real bird," said the sailors.

"We want that albatross.

He is good luck."

29

"It is good luck that I found you,"

said Albert.

"Welcome home, Albert!" said everyone.

The End